KU-264-641

EViL WeaseL

E. Weasel

Hannah Shaw

NEW from Evil Weasel PRODUCTS LTD.

Vanity Mirror
With Weasel photo for admiring ♥♥

Fur Removal Cream
For those unsightly furs, may cause irritation

Eau de Weasel
Awful, musty-smelling aftershave

CALL THE SALES NO: 0979931

EVERYONE NEEDS

Weasel's Evil Practical Joke Kit!

Stinky Bombs

Pencil Catapult

Electrifying Prong

Exploding Cake

Weasel Mask

Cabbage-flavoured sweets

Terrify Your Friends! HA! HA

INVEST YOUR SAVINGS IN THE WEASEL BANK

All your money will be given to *Evil Weasel* Inc.

FLEAS

DELIVERED DIRECT TO YOUR DOOR
NO QUESTIONS ASKED
CALL E. WEASEL: 0979931

- YAK FLEAS FROM MONGOLIA
- HOT! HOT! CHILLI FLEAS
- ORGANIC RARE-BREED FLEAS
- INVISIBLE FLEAS
- REGULAR FLEAS

Many Itchy Uses

Haunted Castle Tour

Spooky!

At Weasel Towers tonight...

Watch out!
Weasel in ghost costume about!

HUNGRY CROCS IN THE MOAT

£20

LAB RAT

Looking for a keen helper to take part in a very important scientific experiment. Must have an interest in cheese. Apply to Rat's laboratory. 0356713

FAT CAT

Wants new home/owner, preferably with large swimming pool. Only eats caviar from a silver dish. Call Mr Tibbles: 06571-287

E. Weasel: If you are reading this, I want an apology. Shrew.

MISSING

4 large, dangerous crocodiles, stolen from the safari park 2 weeks ago. If found do not panic – call Stan's Safari Park.

WEASEL'S AUTOS

Every car is guaranteed to break down as soon as you leave my garage!

USED CARS

MAKE A FORTUNE
from others' Misfortune!

GETTING RICH THE easy WAY

Also by the same author:
I'M BETTER THAN YOU!
E. Weasel - An Autobiography

I'M BETTER THAN YOU!

EAT AT WEASEL BURGER

Unhealthy food, terrible service!

COUPON

1 for 2

MORAY COUNCIL
LIBRARIES &
INFO.SERVICES

20 30 41 98	
Askews	
JA	

For Hairy Toes,
Furry Paws
and Arthur

This book belongs to:

Evil Weasel ESQ

and

EVIL WEASEL
A RED FOX BOOK 978 1 862 30428 4

Published in Great Britain by Jonathan Cape,
an imprint of Random House Children's Books
A Random House Group Company

Jonathan Cape edition published 2008
Red Fox edition published 2009

1 3 5 7 9 10 8 6 4 2

Copyright © Hannah Shaw, 2008

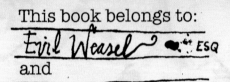

The right of Hannah Shaw to be identified as the author and illustrator of this work
has been asserted in accordance with the Copyright, Designs and Patents Act 1988.

All rights reserved.

Red Fox Books are published by RANDOM HOUSE CHILDREN'S BOOKS
61–63 Uxbridge Road, London W5 5SA

www.kidsatrandomhouse.co.uk
www.rbooks.co.uk

Addresses for companies within The Random House Group Limited
can be found at: www.randomhouse.co.uk/offices.htm

THE RANDOM HOUSE GROUP Limited Reg. No. 954009

A CIP catalogue record for this book is available from the British Library.

Printed in Malaysia

KEEP OFF!

Evil Weasel

Hannah Shaw

RED FOX

Weasel was evil.

He was a bully and a *sneak*
— a nasty, measly, evilly Weasel.

His *mean* schemes and *cunning* tricks
had made him *richer* than
you can possibly imagine.

EVIL IS THE NEW GOOD!

One day Weasel decided to throw a party to boast about his incredible castle, fast car and **huge** swimming pool.

He sent off invitations to everyone he could think of.

invitation

Dear friends,
I, Evil Weasel, invite you —
yes, *you* — to a party.
I am very rich and important,
so don't be late.
Signed,
E. Weasel ✦ ESQ
E. Weasel ESQ. at Weasel Towers
P.S. Watch out, the crocodiles in
the moat might be hungry!

On *the day* of the party
Weasel dressed in his finest clothes
and admired himself in the mirror.

"Don't I look handsome?"
he asked his reflection.

Then Weasel waited expectantly for his guests to arrive.

He waited...

and Waited...

But no one came.

Being rich and powerful isn't much fun when there's no one to impress.

"Why would anyone **not** want to come to my party?" sulked Weasel.

"I will visit them all and demand an explanation."

First, Weasel went to see Rabbit. He banged on the door.
When Rabbit saw Weasel, he started *shaking*.
"What's the matter with *you*?" Said Weasel crossly.
"And why didn't you come to *my* party?"

Rabbit looked a bit upset.

"Don't you remember how mean to me you were at school?" he asked.

"Oh," said Weasel, *r*emembering.

Next, Weasel went to see Rat in his laboratory. "Why didn't you come to my party?" he snapped.

Off Weasel went to visit Hedgehog, but on the way he met Hedgehog's mum. "Hedgehog isn't *very* well," she said.

"He's been scratching for days and days and he just can't stop."

"Ah," said Weasel, feeling a bit itchy himself.

Weasel was starting to feel quite *guilty*,
so he *crept* past Shrew's house.

"Not so *fast*," said a little voice.

Shrew
Recycling

RECYCLE
MORE!

"It was a joke," protested Weasel.
"My cat only likes caviar,
he wouldn't eat you."

"Well it wasn't funny," squeaked Shrew.

"Nobody came to your party because
you're mean and nasty and a bad friend.
And you never ever say sorry!"

Weasel went *home* feeling m*easly*.
He had been a *horrible bully*.

"I *must find* a way to be a *good* friend,"
he thought desperately,

"but h*ow*?"

Weasel paced r**o**u**n**d and r**o**u**n**d all night,
trying to think of good ideas.
This wasn't e**a**sy because
most of *his* thoughts were *wickedly* evil,
but by morning he had a pla**n** . . .

"What I need to do," said Weasel,

"is put right everything I've done wrong."

So that is exactly what he did.

Everyone was pleased that Weasel was making *such* an effort.

"But there is still one thing we *haven't* heard you say," said Shrew.

Weasel thought long and hard. After a while, he began to mumble,

"I'm *so* . . . *so* important! No . . . I'm *su* . . . super evil?"

The other animals began to laugh.

"I've got it!" cried Weasel.

"I'm Sorry!"

"Hurray!" they all cheered.

Weasel decided to throw a party to celebrate being good at being good.

This time, everyone came.

"Yippee!" cried Weasel.

"Let's party!"

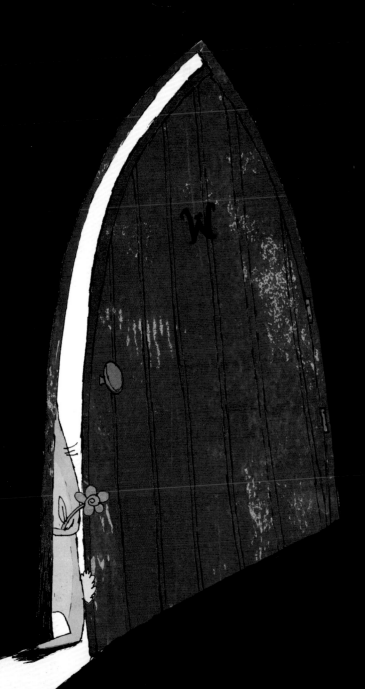

And *I*'d like to say that Weasel *finally* learned
the error of his ways and stopped being *evil* altogether.

But *sometimes* he just couldn't help himself . . .

NEW

from Weasel
PRODUCTS LTD.

Weasel Teddy
Give me a cuddle!

Instant Fur
For those who like the fluffy look!

Happy like Weasel
Fun-to-wear T-shirt

CALL THE SALES NO: 0979931

EVERYONE NEEDS

Flowers

Tickets for a day out
museum admits 1
museum Admits 2

Non-Exploding Cake

Weasel's Nice Surprise Kit!

Happy Snapshot Camera

Thank-you Card

Thanks!

Nice-flavoured sweets

Let Your friends KNOW YOU CARE

FREE MONEY & PIGGY BANK

WEASEL BANK

Money will not be kept in a swimming pool.

ANTI-FLEA SHAMPOO

Gets rid of even the toughest fleas!

Banish fleas!

Party Castle!

Your host will be Weasel

Music & Dancing!
Come and have a good time!

FREE

RABBIT

HUTCH for sale, great views, very nice neighbours and large carrot patch. Call Rabbit today on 4678277

Do you like sweeping up leaves, eating and short country walks? Then you could be the perfect partner for a single lady with prickles. Call Mrs H today: 0384732

Weasel: If you are reading this, I forgive you and would you and Mr Tibbles like to come to tea? Shrew

---

— FOUND —

4 large, dangerous crocodiles. Thank you, Mr Weasel, for their safe return and your generous donation to the safari park.

WEASEL'S BICYCLE REPAIRS

Let me help you! I can mend your bike so it's better than new!

BIKES MENDED

NEW SELF-HELP GUIDES

BEING NICE IS easy! WEASEL

Also by the same author:
BULLYING IS WRONG
Weasel – A self-help book

BULLYING IS WRONG By weasel

self-help book

EAT AT WEASEL'S DELI

Healthy food, great service!

COUPON

2 for 1